Hey, kids!
See if you can spot Santa,
Mrs. Claus, and Reindeer
hidden throughout the story.

To..

You made it onto Santa's NICE list—GOOD JOB!

MERRY CHRISTMAS!

Love, from..

I SAW SANTA IN CHICAGO

Written by J.D. Green

Illustrated by Nadja Sarell and Srimalie Bassani

sourcebooks
jabberwocky

anta's not planned his vacation this year.
Mrs. Claus says, "How 'bout Chicago, my dear?
You always say it's your favorite place,
but remember, the children should not see your face."

"It's true," Santa says. "Chicago has it all:
great sights, tasty bites, fun times great and small."

Mrs. Claus says, "We should set off tonight!
And you heard what I said? You must keep out of sight!"

They load up the sleigh, getting set to explore,
and head off to Chicago, ready for more!
Through Hyde Park, Streeterville, and Wrigleyville they go.
"I love being back!" Santa says. "Ho! Ho! Ho!"

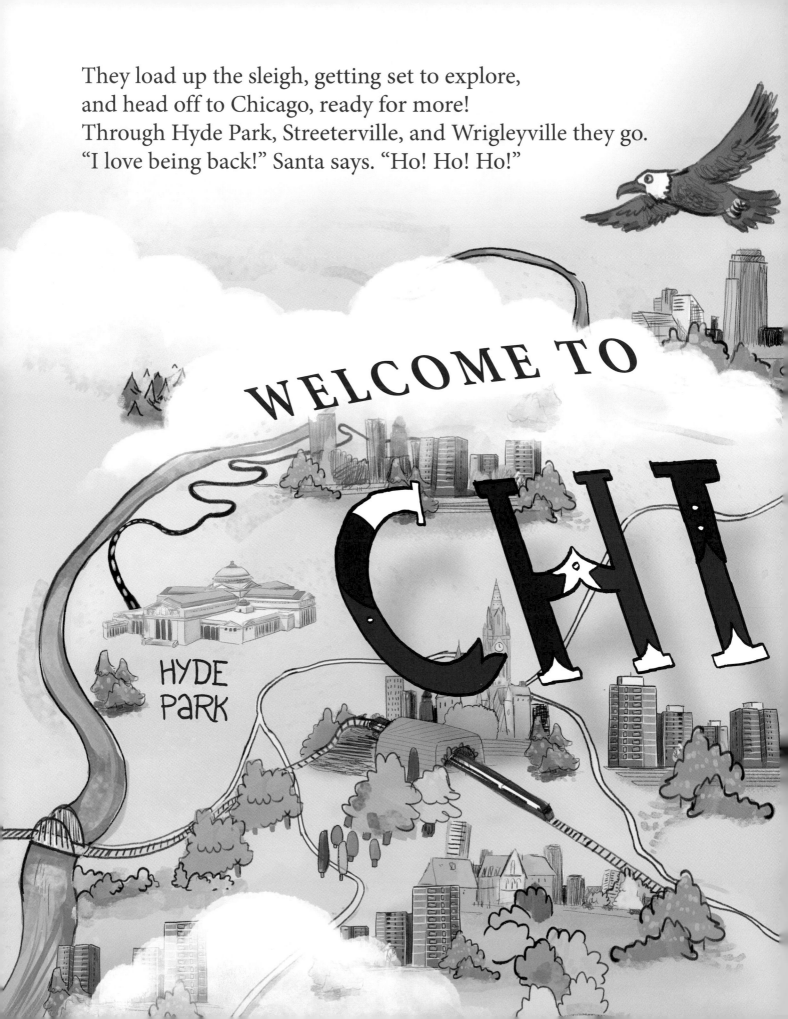

WELCOME TO CHI

HYDE PARK

STREETERVILLE

WRIGLEYVILLE

CAGO

It's a family tradition, when they go away,
to buy a few gifts to remember their stay.

Smart Mrs. Claus came prepared with a list,
so first she'll go shop—not one friend will be missed!

Santa thinks buying nice gifts is quite tough.
He's feeling confused—there's just so much stuff!

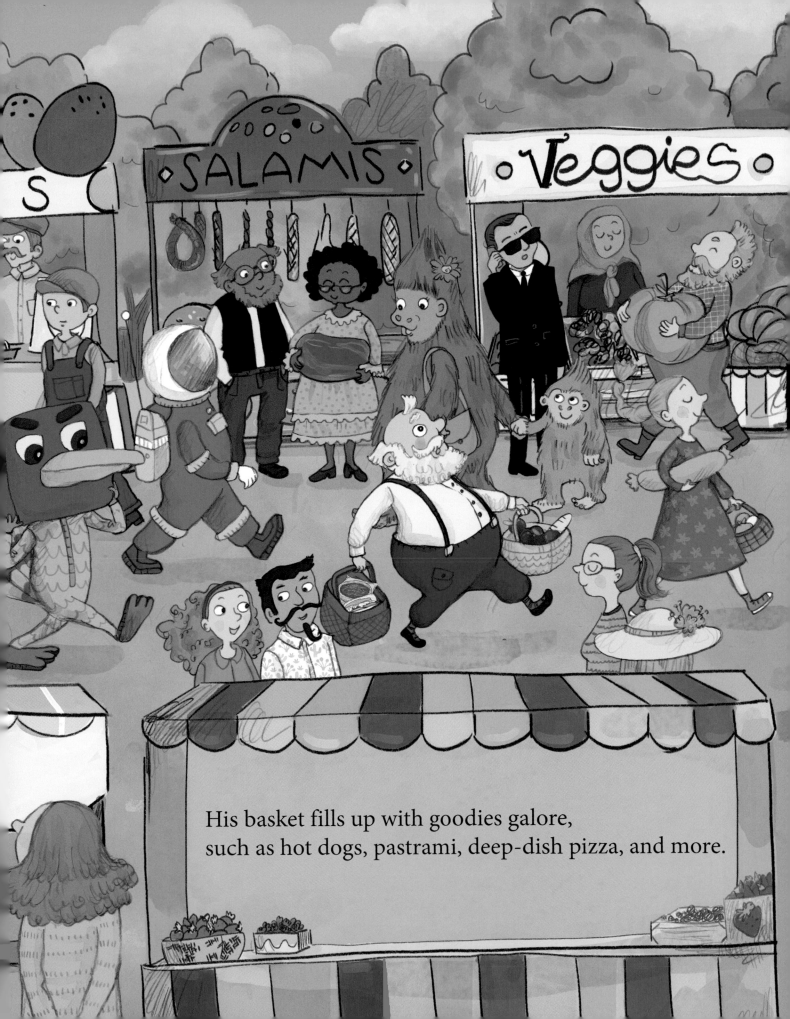

His basket fills up with goodies galore,
such as hot dogs, pastrami, deep-dish pizza, and more.

Reindeer's not eager to stick to plans,
there's so much to see and experience firsthand!

But first he must find a good new disguise,
so he can blend in with the crowd outside!

The Clauses are done with their shopping for friends.
Now it's time to go sightseeing before their trip ends!

Back in the North Pole, Head Elf checks the mail.
He opens one letter and turns very pale…

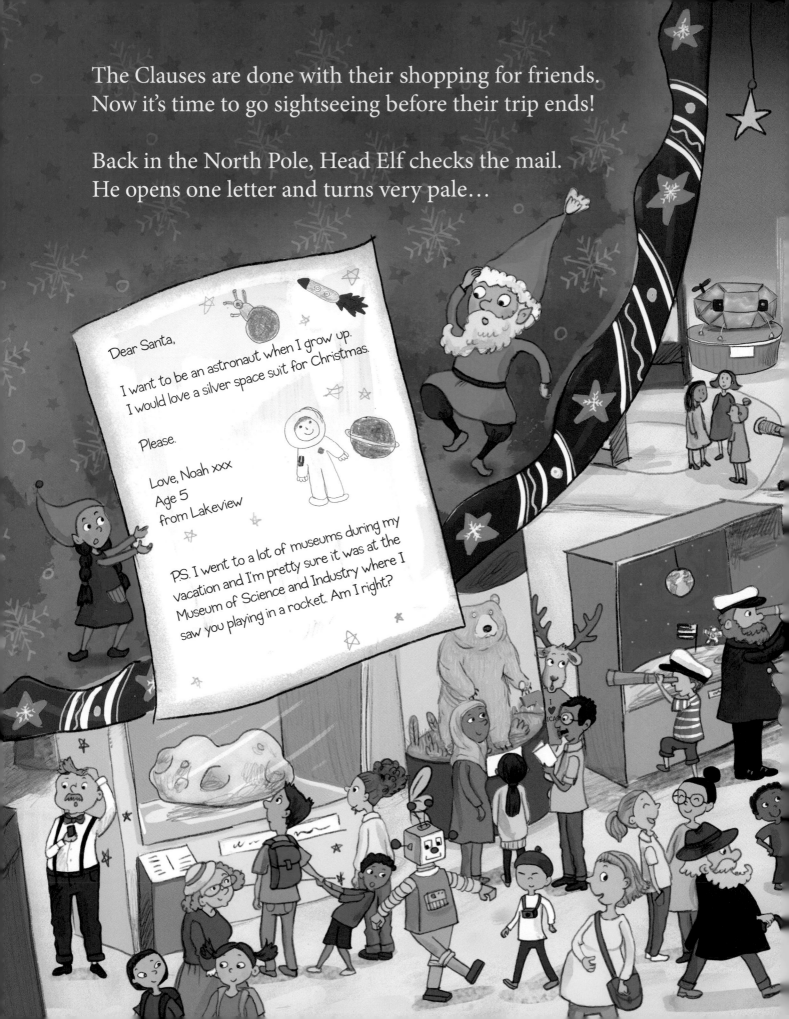

Dear Santa,

I want to be an astronaut when I grow up.
I would love a silver space suit for Christmas.

Please.

Love, Noah xxx
Age 5
from Lakeview

P.S. I went to a lot of museums during my vacation and I'm pretty sure it was at the Museum of Science and Industry where I saw you playing in a rocket. Am I right?

FREEZE-DRIED ASTRONAUT ICE CREAM

EXIT

Dear Santa,

My favorite place in the whole wide world is the ocean! Please can I have a snorkel and flippers for Christmas? Thank you!

By the way, I was at Six Flags Hurricane Harbor yesterday. I didn't have my glasses on while I was swimming, but I saw someone with a big, white beard and a red-and-white bathing suit. Was it you? Please write back and tell me.

Love, Emma
Age 7
from Pilsen

At home in the North, Head Elf says, "This won't do! One sighting is terrible. Now we've had two!"

Santa should really be taking more care.
It seems yet more children have spotted him there.

Dear Santa,

I would love, love, love a big, pink unicorn!
I drew one for you here.

Love, Bella x X x
Age 5¾
from Union Ridge

P.S. Did I see you at Eggers Grove, wearing
green hiking boots and a red-and-white striped
backpack? It even sounded like you were
whistling "Chicago."

Am I right?

EGGERS
GROVE

Reading the mail, Head Elf shakes his head.
This letter has caused him to turn slightly red!

Hey Santa,

Was that you at City Hall?
I was there with my best friend, Ben. I know you
live in the North Pole, but it really looked just like
you sitting on the bench, wearing sunglasses and
drinking a milkshake.

Oh, and we would like new baseball bats for
Christmas, please!

Bye!
William
Age 7
from Dunning

In the North Pole, Head Elf can't believe what he's seeing!
Another TWO children have seen Santa fleeing.

Hello Santa,

My name is Olivia and I am 6½.
I love horseback riding and would like new boots
for Christmas. I went to Naperville Ribfest.

Did you go, too? I'm pretty sure I saw you
riding a horse while eating a hot dog!

Was that really you?

Love, Olivia
from Bucktown

HOT

Hi Santa,

I am 8 and I would like a real duck for Christmas. My grandpa and I were watching the ducks at Lincoln Park when we saw a big, red sleigh on the other side of the pond. I heard the park ranger say sleighs do not float.

Was that you?

James
from Archer Heights

The vacation is over; the shopping is done.
See you soon, Chicago! Thanks for the fun!

THANKS FOR
VISITING
CHICAGO

Upon arriving home, Head Elf lets Santa know he's been spotted by multiple children. Oh no!

Emma, age 7

Noah, age 5

Bella, age 5¾

Dear Noah,
Yes, you did spot me at the
museum! I was on my summer
vacation in Chicago.
Enjoy your silver space suit.
Love, Santa
x

Dear Emma,
Yes, you did spot me at
Six Flags Hurricane Harbor!
Chicago is my favorite
place to visit.
Have fun with your snorkel
and flippers.
Love, Santa
x

Dear Bella,
Yes, you did spot me at
Eggers Grove! I was on
my summer vacation in
Chicago.
Have fun with your pink
unicorn!
Love, Santa
x

Mrs. Claus and Santa know just what to do.
They'll clean up this mess with a special gift or two.

When Christmas arrives, all the children who wrote
get one EXTRA gift, and inside is a note…

To my favorite child in Chicago.

On my summer break, I like getting away,
so I go to Chicago, the best place to stay.
There's so much in Chicago that I like to see,
there really is no place that I'd rather be.

So be on the lookout, 'cuz you never know,
if I might be somewhere that you like to go.
And if you have time, I like nothing better
than hearing from YOU! So write me a letter!

Merry Christmas!

Love,
Santa
XXX

Written by J.D. Green
Illustrated by Nadja Sarell and Srimalie Bassani
Additional art by Darran Holmes
Designed by Geff Newland

Published by Sourcebooks Jabberwocky, an imprint of Sourcebooks, Inc.
P.O. Box 4410, Naperville, Illinois 60567-4410
(630) 961-3900
Fax: (630) 961-2168
jabberwockykids.com

Date of Production: August 2018
Run Number: HTW_PO201802
Printed and bound in China (GD)
10 9 8 7 6 5 4 3 2 1